Cambridge Early Years

Communication and Language
for English as a Second Language

Learner's Book 3C

Claire Medwell

Contents

Note to parents and practitioners — 3

Block 5: How things work — 4

Block 6: Space and the future — 19

Acknowledgements — 32

Note to parents and practitioners

This Learner's Book provides activities to support the third term of ESL Communication and Language for Cambridge Early Years 3.

Activities can be used at school or at home. Children will need support from an adult. Additional guidance about activities can be found in the **For practitioners** boxes.

Stories are provided for children to enjoy looking at and listening to. Children are not expected to be able to read the stories themselves.

Children will encounter the following characters within this book. You could ask children to point to the characters when they see them on the pages, and say their names.

The Learner's Book activities support the Teaching Resource activities. The Teaching Resource provides step-by-step coverage of the Cambridge Early Years curriculum and guidance on how the Learner's Book activities develop the curriculum learning statements.

Hi, my name is Mia.

Find us on the front covers doing lots of fun activities.

Hi, my name is Gemi.

Hi, my name is Rafi.

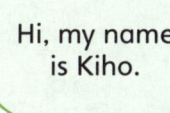

Hi, my name is Kiho.

Block 5 — How things work

I Did Too! by Alex Eeles

Do you want to know something AMAZING?
My Uncle Ali is an explorer.
Not the kind you find in books either.
An actual real-life explorer!

He travels all over the world
to visit incredible places
and see incredible things.

Wherever he goes, he always sends me a postcard!

Like when he crossed the Amazon jungle in Brazil …

and I did too!

When he ate a pizza in Italy …

and I did too!

When he found a shipwreck in South Africa ...

and I did too!

7

When he climbed a mountain in Nepal …

and I did too!

When he rode a camel in Egypt ...
escaped a bear in Canada ...
and raced a kangaroo in Australia ...

and I did too!

He even walked along the Great Wall of China.

And guess what?

I DID TOO!

Picture postcard

Read and say.

Read the postcard and use the pictures to say the correct words. Write the word under each picture.

I'm in Brazil with my *family*. It's hot and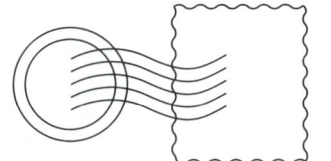

sunny. I have lunch at *1 o'clock*

and then I go *fishing* with my sister. In the

afternoon we collect *shells* on the beach.

For practitioners
Invite children to read the postcard and to say the missing words with the help of the pictures. If able, children can trace the missing words in the space provided, with your help and guidance.

I Did Too!

Listen and trace.

Listen to the story and trace the route.

For practitioners
Encourage children to look at the postcards and identify what they can see. Invite them to form simple sentences about the pictures and to predict Uncle Ali's journey. Then children listen to the story and mark the route with a pencil line.

My favourite place

Draw and say.

Draw your favourite place on the postcard. Talk about it.

For practitioners
Encourage children to talk about their favourite place. This could be in their town or city or a holiday destination. Invite them to describe their chosen place using simple words and phrases, and to talk about the activities they do there, e.g., *At the animal sanctuary, I feed the animals.*

We've Got the Whole World in Our Hands

(Traditional children's song)

We've got the whole world in our hands,
We've got the whole world in our hands,
We've got the whole world in our hands,
We've got the whole world in our hands,

Other verses:

We've got our friends and our family in our hands …
We've got our brothers and our sisters in our hands …
We've got the sun and the rain in our hands …
We've got the moon and the stars in our hands …
We've got the winds and the clouds in our hands …
We've got the rivers and mountains in our hands …
We've got the sea and oceans in our hands …
We've got the towns and cities in our hands …

The world around us

Read and circle.

Look at each picture.
Read and circle the correct word.

family   friends

brothers   sisters

sun   rain

moon   stars

wind   clouds

river   mountains

village   city

For practitioners
Ask children to identify the different words under the pictures. Encourage them to use *This is …* and *These are …* for the singular and plural nouns. Ask children to read and circle the word that describes each picture, offering support if necessary.

The whole world

Listen and draw.

Listen to the song.
Draw lines to match the words that go together.

For practitioners
Invite children to identify the different elements they can see in the pictures. Remind them of the song and encourage them to predict the words that go together. Help support their understanding by providing an example, e.g., *friends and family*. Encourage the use of *and* to link words.

My world

Look and draw.

Look at the pictures and choose which ones to draw in your world.

For practitioners
Invite children to design their own world using the small nature illustrations as inspiration. Encourage them to think independently by drawing their own ideas. Prompt them to talk about their pictures using simple words and expressions.

Block 6 Space and the future

Tak's Space Trip by Alex Eeles

Tak is feeling nervous,
she rushes to get dressed.
Today, she has to fly to space
to pass her final test!

She climbs into her spaceship,
and sits down in her chair.
She listens to the countdown,
and BLASTS OFF into the air!

10 9 8 7 6 5 4 3 2 1 LIFT OFF!

Tak travels at the speed of light,
across the Milky Way.
She takes a selfie on the moon,
what will her friends all say?

She steers between the space rocks,
and through the shooting stars.
She visits a space station,
that's floating next to Mars!

She passes giant Jupiter,
and Saturn with its rings.
She stops in at Uranus
and meets an alien king!

Tak turns the ship at Neptune,
and starts the journey back.
She eats up all the space snacks,
that she keeps inside her pack!

She soars across the galaxy,
and sees the Earth at last.
Blue and green upon her screen,
Tak's home! But has she passed?

Her friends are waiting on the ground.
They watch her as she lands.
They smile when she walks down the steps …

… then cheer and clap their hands!

Mr Sakaguchi gives Tak her medal and pins it to her chest.
Space School's newest pilot.
Where will she fly to next?

Planets

Read and colour.

Read the sentences. Colour the planets to match.

1   It is red.

2   It has rings.
    It is yellow.

3 It is blue and green.

4 It has orange and red stripes.

For practitioners
Children read the sentences and then colour each planet to match its description. Point to and read the words for children who require support. Ask them which planet we live on and challenge them to find it in the story text. Teach the names of the other planets mentioned in the text and encourage children to match them with the planets they have coloured in.

My spaceship

Trace and colour.

Trace and colour your spaceship.
Draw a picture of yourself inside.

For practitioners

Ask children to predict what the picture is and then trace the outline of their spaceship. Children colour it in and draw themselves inside. Encourage them to describe their picture. Ask children where they would fly to first.

True or false?

Circle and say.

Circle the pictures from the story.
Say what you see.

For practitioners
Ask children questions about the context of each image, e.g., *Is Tak flying her spaceship? Is Tak watching television?* Children show an understanding of the simple questions and story context by circling the correct pictures from the story.

Five Little Aliens

Five little aliens flew to space
(wiggle your hand in the air)

The first one said, "Let's have a race!"
(hold up your thumb to indicate first)

The second one flew past Neptune
(hold up your thumb and one finger)

The third one landed on the moon
(hold up your thumb and two fingers)

The fourth one flew past the sun
(hold up your thumb and three fingers)

And the fifth one said, "Yippee! I've won!"
(hold up thumb and four fingers, then wave your hands in the air)

Five Little Aliens

Join the dots.

Join the dots to complete the picture.

For practitioners
Encourage children to describe the aliens in the picture. Prompt them with questions, such as *How many aliens are there? Is one wearing a bow?* Invite them to guess what the missing elements are, before they join the dots and colour the picture.

Ready, steady, go!

Spot the difference.

Find and circle the differences in the pictures.

For practitioners

Ask children to observe the two pictures illustrating the rhyme. They might like to sing the rhyme from memory. Explain that the pictures look similar but encourage them to find and circle the differences. Ask questions, e.g., *Do they fly past Saturn? Does the spaceship land on the moon?*

My alien

Draw and say.

Draw your own alien.
Say where it is going in its spaceship.

For practitioners

Explain to children that there is a sixth alien, which is going to be their alien.
Ask them to draw and describe it using simple phrases and to choose a planet to visit.
Encourage children to respond to *why* questions about their choices using simple words.

Acknowledgements

The authors and publishers acknowledge the following sources of copyright material and are grateful for the permissions granted. While every effort has been made, it has not always been possible to identify the sources of all the material used, or to trace all copyright holders. If any omissions are brought to our notice, we will be happy to include the appropriate acknowledgements on reprinting.

Thanks to the following for permission to reproduce images:

p24 Jakkrapat/Getty Images, p31 Tamiris6/Getty Images

Thanks to the following artists at Beehive Illustration:

Lays Bittencourt, Tamara Joubert, John Lund, Michelle McGovern, Claire Philpott, Sarah Pitt.

Cover characters by Becky Davies (The Bright Agency)